This Orchard book belongs to:

_____

_____

_____

_____

For Amy, Mum and my super brother, Andy.

ORCHARD BOOKS
First published in Great Britain in 2016 by The Watts Publishing Group
This edition first published in 2016
3 5 7 9 10 8 6 4
Text and illustrations © Matt Robertson, 2016
The moral rights of the author have been asserted. All rights reserved.
A CIP catalogue record for this book is available from the British Library.
ISBN 978 1 40833 729 5 • Printed and bound in China

MIX
Paper from
responsible sources
FSC
www.fsc.org
FSC® C104740

Orchard Books
An imprint of Hachette Children's Group
Part of The Watts Publishing Group Limited
Carmelite House, 50 Victoria Embankment, London EC4Y 0DZ
An Hachette UK Company
www.hachette.co.uk
www.hachettechildrens.co.uk

SUPER STAN

Matt Robertson

ORCHARD

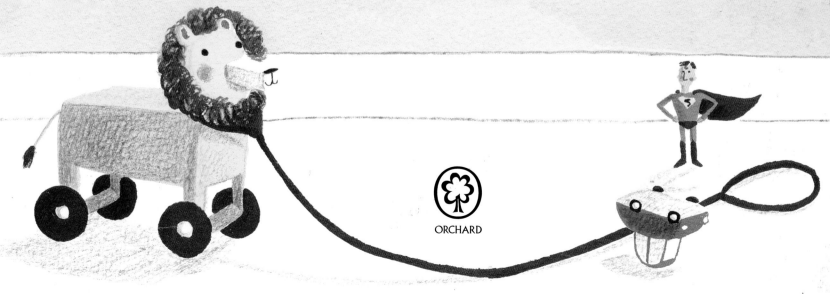

Jack and Stan were brothers.

JACK

They were very different.

STAN

Stan could always run FASTER...

...throw FURTHER...

...and jump HIGHER.

Oh, and Stan could also . . .

...FLY!

Whenever Jack did something ordinary,

Stan did something EXTRAordinary.

Whenever Jack did something good,

Stan did something AMAZING!

The whole world thought
Stan was super . . .

. . . except Jack.

Jack was tired of always being second best.

On Jack's birthday,
his special treat was
a trip to the zoo.

He didn't want anything
to spoil his day.

"Please don't ruin my birthday treat, Stan," said Jack.

But Stan was far too excited to listen.

Before long, Stan was racing the CHEETAHS...

. . . wrestling a

LION...

...and playing with the GIRAFFES.

Everyone clapped and cheered . . .

... except Jack.

"This was supposed to be
MY special day,"
Jack thought sadly.

But then Jack heard a sound.

Stan sniffed . . .
his lip wobbled . . .
and then he let out a SUPER scream.

"WAAAAAAAAA"

The crying got
LOUDER and
LOUDER.

giraffe

ball

Stan

bear

teddy

Nobody knew
what was wrong
. . . except Jack.

Because, after all,
he was Stan's big
brother.

As quick as a flash,
Jack sprang into action!

And just . . .

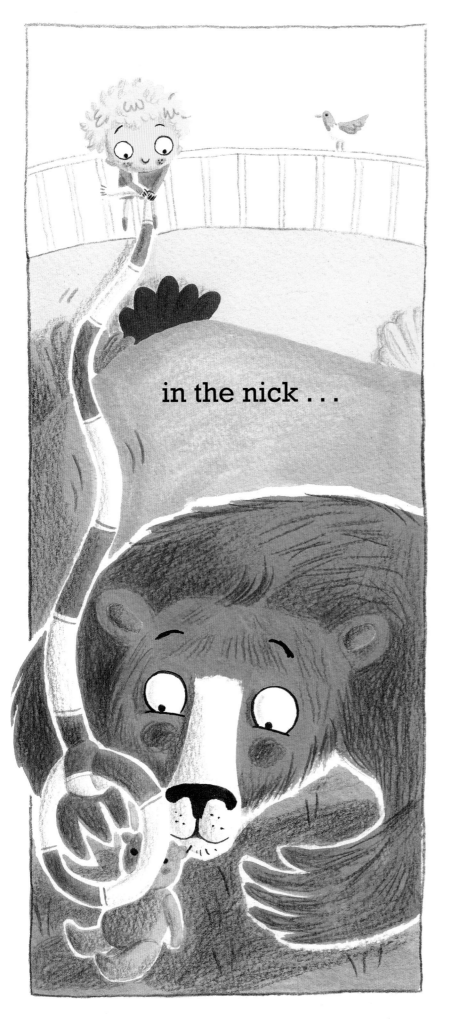

in the nick . . .

of TIME . . .

...JACK

SAVED THE DAY!

After all, that's what big brothers do.

Stan stopped crying and gave Jack a

SUPER hug.

Jack felt like a real super hero!

And from that day on, Jack and Stan were

SUPER BROTHERS!

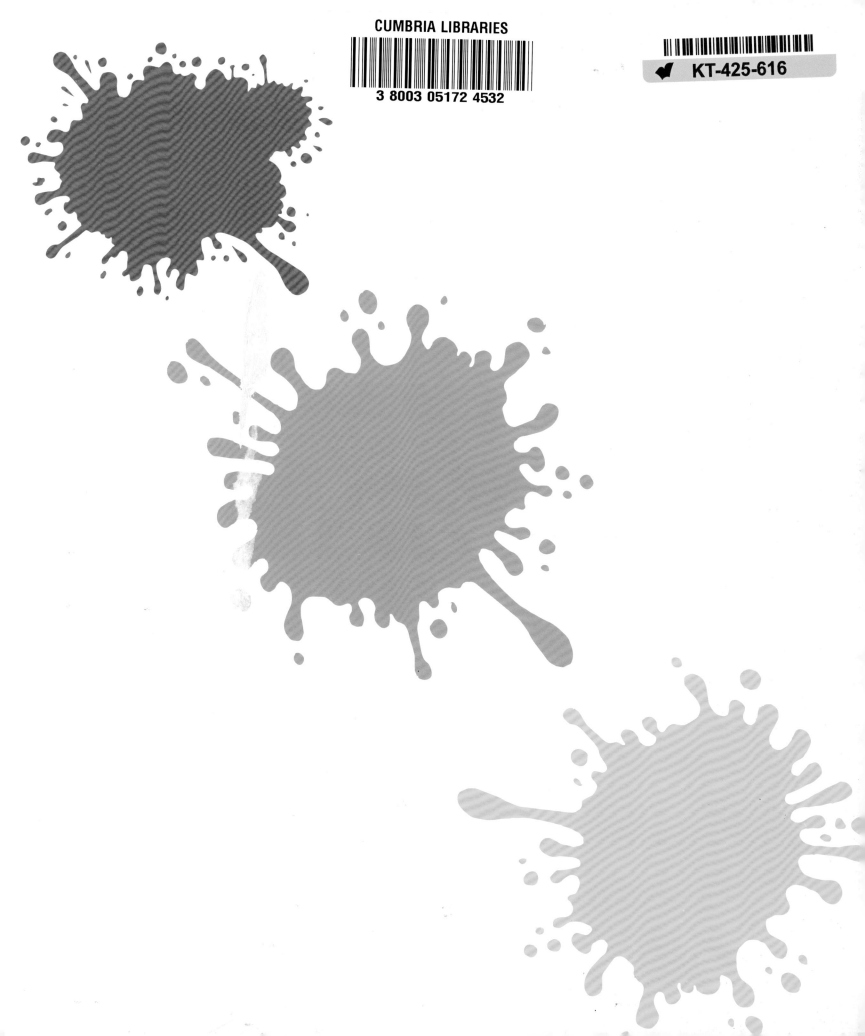

For Ring.
M.C.

First published in Great Britain 2020 by Egmont UK Limited
2 Minster Court, 10th Floor, London EC3R 7BB

www.egmont.co.uk

Text and Illustrations © Matt Carr 2020

Matt Carr has asserted his moral rights.

ISBN 978 1 4052 9688 5

A CIP catalogue record for this title is available from the British Library.

RHINOCORN
RULES!

Matt Carr

EGMONT

Ron looked the same as any other rhinoceros.
He was big, he was grey and he had
a pointy thing on the top of his nose.

But Ron *felt* different.

Now, Ron knew the **THREE RHINO RULES . . .**

Rule 1: Be alone.

Rule 2: Be a bit grumpy.

Rule 3: Charge at anything that comes near you.

He loved **FUN,**
ART, LAUGHTER and **MUSIC!**
He was just bursting
with **IDEAS** and **JOY!**

Ron wanted to share this with everyone, but because he was a rhino, none of the other animals would go near him.

It's a rhino! Run!

And when he did meet up with another rhino,
they didn't want to chat . . .

they just wanted to **CHARGE!**

Life wasn't much fun
for poor Ron . . .

until one hot afternoon
at the watering hole,
when he looked at his
grey reflection in the water.

"If only I could show
everyone my **TRUE COLOURS**,"
he thought. "Then I'd be sure
to make friends."

This gave Ron
a great idea!

First, he rolled around
in the dust until he was
completely covered in it.

The sticky colours soon dried in the hot sun.
Ron was a walking **WORK OF ART!**

He felt

A-MA-ZING!

The meerkats were the first to notice Ron. Instead of running away, they all gathered around him. They were very impressed by this colourful new animal.

"ARE YOU A UNICORN?"

asked one of the meerkat pups.

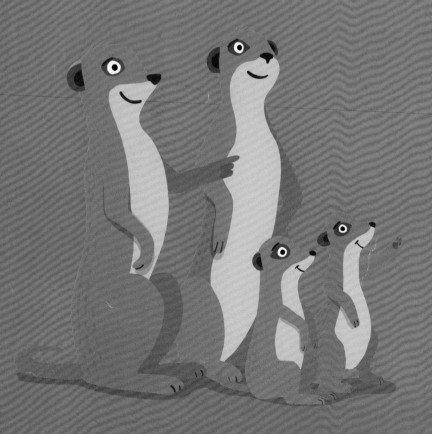

Ron thought about it for a moment.
"ER, NO . . . I'M A RHINOCORN!"

The other animals were very excited to meet Ron.

He made lots of new friends . . .

and had lots of **FUN!**

For the first time in his life . . .

Nice throw!

Ron was
HAPPY!

But word of **RON THE RHINOCORN** soon spread . . .

and the other rhinos weren't at all happy!

Ron felt terribly sad.
All he wanted was to make
friends and have fun.

Now he just felt
silly for breaking
the rhino rules.

But Ron's new meerkat pals
were having none of it!

"As long as you're happy with who
you are, that's all that counts!"

The brave little meerkats stood up
for Ron and made a very good point.

"Look at you, all together,
and all getting on with each other,"
they laughed. "Looks like you've
ALL BROKEN THE RHINO RULES!"

It slowly dawned on the other rhinos
that they *had* broken their own rules.

One by one they started to laugh.

"You're right," they agreed.
"We have enjoyed hanging out together!"

"I think it's time we had some **NEW RULES!**" said Ron and he ripped up *The Rhino Rule Book!*

(It wasn't that difficult as it was very thin!)

And so Ron created three much-better rules for everyone to follow . . .

Rule 1: **Be yourself.**

MEERKAT CREATIVE
Paint Service
NO JOB TOO BIG!

Rule 2: **Make lots of friends.**

Rule 3: Have FUN!

And that's exactly what they did!

DID YOU RHI-KNOW?

Even though rhinos are huge they are **HERBIVORES** and only feed on plants.

Rhinos don't get together much but when they do it's called a **CRASH!**

White rhinos are actually grey! They weigh the same as **30 PEOPLE!**

Male rhinos mark out their territory with **POO!**

There are **5** different kinds of rhino: white, black, Sumatran, Javan and Indian.

The word **RHINOCEROS** means **'NOSE HORN'**.

Rhino horns are made out of the same stuff as your fingernails!

Sadly, rhinos are one of the most endangered species on Earth. The main threat to these amazing animals is illegal hunting.
Find out how you can help protect them at:
www.worldwildlife.org

This Little Tiger book belongs to:

_____

_____

_____

For Atticus, with love
~ M C B

For Lilly, with love
~ F E

LITTLE TIGER PRESS
An imprint of Magi Publications
1 The Coda Centre, 189 Munster Road, London SW6 6AW
www.littletigerpress.com

First published in Great Britain 2010
This edition published 2011

A CIP catalogue record for this book is available from the British Library

Printed in China

LTP/1800/0206/0511

2 4 6 8 10 9 7 5 3 1

The First Snow

M Christina Butler   Frank Endersby

LITTLE TIGER PRESS
London

Little Deer peeped out of his bed and blinked
in the morning sunshine.

"Yikes!" he squeaked. "Where's everything gone?"

Everywhere looked different. The wood was covered
with a huge white blanket.

Just then, Rabbit came skidding over,
shouting, "Snow! Snow! Look at the snow!"
    "Yippeee!" Squirrel cried, jumping out
of a pine tree.

"What's happened?" squeaked Little Deer.
"Where's all the grass gone?"

"It's under the snow," giggled Rabbit, beginning to dig. "Ta-daah!" he said as a tuft of icy grass appeared.

Little Deer nibbled a bit here and nibbled a bit there. The cold, crispy grass was very strange.

On and on they twirled until the moon shone
bright, and stars twinkled in the deep blue sky.
Little Deer's first snow had been such a
surprise, but it had been the best fun ever!

"Hurray!" shouted Little
  Deer, up on his feet at last.
"Let's skate!"

Slowly and slippily, wibbling and wobbling, they tried to stand up . . .

BUMP!

 **SWOOSH!**

THUMP!

They skidded and slipped, and down they fell again and again!
"Bother!" squeaked Squirrel.
"Eeek!" giggled Rabbit.

SWOOSH! They skimmed off the bottom of the hillside, spun across the ice and landed, CRASH! in a big, snowy heap.

"That was awesome!" gasped Little Deer, as they all shook off the snow.

Slipping and sliding, they all chased
down the hill. Faster and faster the
snowball rolled, and faster and faster
they tumbled after it . . .

and soon it was so big they
couldn't push it any further!

"Let's make the snowman a head!" said Squirrel.
"He'll be bigger than me!" Little Deer laughed.
But with a creak and a groan the snowball began
to roll down the hillside.
"Oh no!" shouted Little Deer. "Stop that snowman!"

These Little Tiger books are the best fun ever!

For information regarding any of the above titles or for our catalogue, please contact us:
Little Tiger Press, 1 The Coda Centre, 189 Munster Road, London SW6 6AW
Tel: 020 7385 6333 • Fax: 020 7385 7333 • E-mail: info@littletiger.co.uk • www.littletigerpress.com